Mermaids
TO THE RESCUE

Nixie Makes Waves

ALSO BY LISA ANN SCOTT

Mermaids TO THE RESCUE

The Wish Fairy

ENCHANTED PONY ACADEMY

Mermaids

TO THE RESCUE

Nixie Makes Waves

Lisa Ann Scott

illustrated by
Heather Burns

SCHOLASTIC INC.

Text copyright © 2019 by Lisa Ann Scott
Illustrations by Heather Burns, © 2019 Scholastic Inc.

ISBN 978-1-338-26697-9

10 9 8 7 6 5 4 3 2 1   19 20 21 22 23

Printed in the U.S.A.   40

First printing 2019

Book design by Yaffa Jaskoll

To Aunt Diane,
I know we're both long-lost mermaids.
Love you!

Chapter 1

Princess Nixie flicked her shiny rainbow tail back and forth like she always did when she was trying to solve a problem. She called her method "swishing a fix"—usually it just took a few swirls of her tail to find a clever solution to any problem.

But now, she didn't know what to do! *Breathe, focus, solve*, she reminded herself. That's what they practiced at Rescue Crew School when facing a tough situation.

"What's wrong?" her friend Princess Cali asked as they waited backstage at the Oyster Dome arena. "You should be excited. It's finally Selection Day!"

"I know. But I'm not sure which seapony to choose," Nixie said.

Five royal merchildren from all across the Eastern Kingdoms had come to Astoria City, the capital of Astoria Kingdom, Nixie's home. They'd each pick a magical seapony from the Enchanted Seapony Academy. After the Match Ceremony the next day, they'd be official members of the Royal Mermaid Rescue Crew. Nixie got chills just thinking about it.

The seaponies and merchildren would work as partners to keep the seas safe. They'd also live together in the royal merchildren's castles. Rescue Crew partners were always close friends.

"We've been working with the seaponies for a year. And you still don't know who to pick?" Cali asked.

Nixie shrugged. "None of them seem like a perfect match."

Nixie knew the seaponies well. They came from across the Eastern Kingdoms, too, and attended the Enchanted Seapony Academy in Astoria. The seaponies and merchildren worked together at Rescue Crew School on the weekends.

"I want to choose Rio," Cali said. "She has such a great Sea Savvy. Blowing a big protection bubble will come in handy. And we got along really well during our training sessions."

"I don't know which seapony is the right match for me," Nixie said. "But I know who's not—Rip."

"But he's so fast." Cali's twin brother, Prince Cruise, swam up to join them. "And he's a super cool shade of blue."

"Then why don't *you* pick him?" Nixie asked.

Cruise laughed. "Because he's bossy and doesn't know how to have fun."

Princess Lana joined them. "Remember how mad he got when you did your fish presentation on jellyfish?" she reminded Nixie.

"Of course. Because 'jellyfish aren't fish'!" Nixie swished her tail again. "But they're awesome. And they have the word *fish* in their name. That counts."

"And you taught them how to dance to your singing!" Cali said.

Nixie smiled. She *had* been proud of that presentation.

"I hear he always has a copy of the rule book in his saddlebag," Prince Dorado said, swimming up.

While her friends were laughing, Nixie bit her lip. "Guys, we shouldn't be so mean. He tries hard. He's great at playing fetch. And he has top marks in his class."

"We're not being mean. It's the truth," Cruise said. "He wouldn't be a very fun partner."

Nixie had to agree about that.

Nixie imagined the thrill she would feel working with exactly the right seapony. Her heart sped up just thinking about it. But none of the five seaponies in this year's selection class gave her that excited feeling. Her teachers always said, "A team takes two." But who did she want on her team?

She swished her tail faster and faster. What was she going to do?

Chapter 2

Nixie snuck a peek at the crowd gathered in the arena to watch the ceremony. The stadium was filled with families of sea-ponies and merfolk. Even dolphins and sea turtles who lived nearby had turned out to watch. The Rescue Crew helped creatures of all kinds, so the ceremony was a popular event.

Nixie's parents, the king and queen of Astoria, and Nixie's sister, Princess Cascadia, were in the front row. Cascadia was two years older and had already gone through the whole selection process. Her seapony, Periwinkle, could conjure whirlpools. Amazing!

Nixie scanned the crowd for her best friends, Piper and Shelby, but she didn't see them. Where could they be?

"Smile. Everything will be fine," Cali said. "Tomorrow we have the Match Ceremony to look forward to. We'll be official Rescue Crew members!"

"Don't forget the party! And presents!" Cruise added. "It's a whole weekend of fun."

"I can't wait to show my seapony how I decorated their room!" Lana said.

"That will be great," Nixie said. It was tradition for the royal merchildren to decorate their new seaponies' rooms before they moved in. Nixie had spent a long time preparing the room next to hers, but she had no idea who'd be living in it after tomorrow!

Just then, Principal Vanora swam backstage. "Children, it's time to begin. Follow me."

She led them onto the stage and the crowd cheered. The seaponies were swimming in from the other side.

Principal Vanora swam to the middle of the stage, holding out a box of big pearls. The students each picked one and waited to look—each pearl had a number that would determine their selection order.

The cold weight of the pearl in Nixie's hand made her nervous.

"Students, find the number marked on your pearl," the principal finally said.

"I got number one!" Cruise shouted.

Nixie slowly uncurled her fingers and stared at the number five. She was going to be last to choose. Now she wasn't going to have a choice at all! She'd be stuck with the last seapony left.

Chapter 3

Nixie forced herself to smile. Hundreds of merboys and girls were watching, and she knew she had to set a good example.

The principal tapped the conch-a-phone so everyone could hear her. "Welcome, families and students. I'm Principal Vanora of the Royal Mermaid Rescue Crew School."

"And I'm Headmaster Caspian of the Enchanted Seapony Academy," said a bright orange seapony.

"We are here today to continue a tradition hundreds of years old," Principal Vanora said.

The headmaster continued with the familiar tale: "Years ago, the powerful magic of our world was weakened by careless spells, both in the earth kingdoms and here below the sea. During this Age of Recklessness, a deep rift formed, splitting the eastern and western waters."

"That created the Great Storm, which swept away so many things, including the Trident of Protection," Principal Vanora said. "The magical blue Sea Diamond, the Fathom Pearl, and the Night Star were lost forever, along with the trident, and the safety it brought to our community."

"And so, the royal merfolk and the magical seaponies joined forces to keep our seas and subjects safe," the headmaster said.

"Choosing a perfect partner is one of the most important tasks a royal mermaid will perform," Principal Vanora told the crowd.

Nixie's heart swelled with pride as she remembered how important this duty was.

Being a merprincess wasn't just crowns and gowns.

"Let's meet our magical seaponies!" Headmaster Caspian said.

Nixie wondered if they were feeling just as nervous as she was.

"Marina is from a long line of magical seaponies," the headmaster said. "Her parents both spent years on the Rescue Crew." The sparkly seapony's fins created swirls of glitter as she swam across the stage. Only sparkly seaponies were magical. Marina seemed like she was covered in jewels. "And watch her marvelous Sea Savvy!"

As everyone watched, Marina's scales

changed color until she blended in with the background onstage. The crowd cheered.

"That will certainly come in handy on rescue missions," the headmaster said.

Nixie touched the help shell that hung on a chain around her neck. Every merperson in the Eastern Kingdoms wore one. That's how they called the Rescue Crew in times of need. But tomorrow, she'd be wearing a bigger rescue shell instead so that she could *receive* the calls. She needed the perfect partner. Her stomach felt like it was swirling with minnows, she was so nervous. She repeated the Rescue Crew motto to herself: *On my honor, I will be brave as I keep our seas and subjects safe.* Just thinking the familiar phrase calmed her down a bit.

"Next, meet Rip!" said the headmaster.

Rip raised his snout and swam to the center of the stage.

"Rip is the oldest of thirty children, and the first member of his family to attend the academy," Headmaster Caspian said.

Three rows of seaponies in the middle of the stadium rose and cheered.

"Rip's magic gave him an amazing Sea Savvy. He's the fastest seapony we've ever had at our school," the headmaster said.

Rip zoomed offstage, swam over the crowd, and returned in seconds.

Shouts and applause filled the stadium.

"Rip also has top marks in his class," the headmaster said.

Rip looked very proud as he returned to the line.

The other magical seaponies were introduced and showed off their Sea Savvies, too.

Once they were finished, Principal Vanora swam to the conch-o-phone. "Royal mermaids, it is time for you to select your Rescue Crew partners. Choose wisely to make the perfect match. Prince Cruise of Coquina, you are first to decide."

Rip smiled and fanned out his fins.

Cruise swam up to a red-and-black-speckled seapony. "I choose Jetty! He blows stun bubbles and he's super cool!"

Rip's smile fell a bit.

"Congratulations, Jetty and Cruise," Headmaster Caspian said. "May you both keep our seas and subjects safe."

"Princess Cali of Coquina, it is your turn," the principal said.

Cali squeezed Nixie's hand and swam up to Rio, a gorgeous purple-and-pink seapony with flowing fins. "You're the perfect seapony for me!" She threw her arms around Rio, and the seapony said, "I was hoping you'd pick me!"

"Princess Lana of Stillwater, come make your selection," Principal Vanora said.

She'll probably pick Rip, Nixie thought.

But Lana swam over to Marina. "I choose you!" Lana said.

"I'm so happy!" Marina bobbed her head.

Rip's eyes were wide. He looked confused.

Dorado was the last royal merchild to choose before Nixie. She crossed her fingers. *Please pick Rip, please pick Rip.*

"Prince Dorado of Shellington, please make your choice," Principal Vanora said.

He swam up to Laguna and said, "We are going to be unstoppable!"

"Woo-hoo!" Laguna said, whipping out her long tail like a lasso. The crowd cheered and laughed.

Nixie wanted to cry, but Rip looked even

sadder. She couldn't let him know how dis-appointed she was.

So before the principal even called her name, she swam over to him. She forced a great big smile and said, "I'm so excited! You're the partner I was hoping to choose! The best in the whole seapony class!"

Chapter 4

Rip's frown turned into a grin. "Really? I never imagined you'd want to pick me. We're very different."

Nixie wasn't sure what to say, because he was right! "Well, sometimes that can be a good thing," she said hopefully.

"Congratulations to our new Rescue Crew teams," Principal Vanora told the crowd. "Join us tomorrow for the official Match Ceremony and party!"

The seaponies and merchildren swam offstage to find their families.

"Congratulations!" Nixie's father, King Zale, said.

Her mother, Queen Avisa, hugged her. "Are you happy?"

Nixie smiled. "Sure." She didn't want to worry them.

"Good. Now go off and have fun with your friends and your new partner!" her mom said.

Her sister, Cascadia, pulled her aside. "What's wrong? I know you're upset."

Nixie quickly told her why Rip was the last seapony she wanted to pick.

Cascadia bit her lip. "Maybe I shouldn't tell you this . . ."

"What?"

"If you're truly that unhappy, you could tell Principal Vanora you don't want to go through with the ceremony tomorrow. You could pick a different pony on the next Selection Day."

"But that's a year from now!" Nixie said. "And Rip would be devastated."

"Your feelings count, too," Cascadia said.

"I know," Nixie said. "But I've never met a problem I couldn't fix. Sometimes, you just have to be creative."

Cascadia laughed. "You certainly know how to do that. Like the time we were swimming through the underwater falls and your pearl necklace broke. You got a starfish to hold it together until we got home. Genius! You swished a fix!"

Nixie smiled and flicked her tail. She loved coming up with smart solutions. "I'll swish a fix for this, too. I'll spend time with Rip today. Maybe we'll get along better than I thought."

"I hope so. Backing out of a selection hardly ever happens, but I just wanted you to know it was an option."

Nixie nodded. "Thanks. I'll see you later."

Cascadia gave her a big hug, and Nixie joined the seaponies and royal merchildren gathered by the stage.

"Let's go celebrate!" Prince Dorado said.

"Follow me, I've got a great idea!" Marina said.

The merchildren and their new partners followed her away from the stadium and the seashell buildings to the outskirts of the city. They swam to the dead zone. This section of coral reef had been destroyed in the Great Storm. Over the years, the coral had died. It was now bleached white, ghostly and quiet. Nixie didn't come back here very often. It was spooky.

Marina stopped in front of a huge coral archway. "Let's go through and visit the river at the Enchanted Pony Academy! I promised Daisy and the other ponies that I'd check in after the ceremony."

Yes! Maybe if we have an adventure together, Rip and I will become friends, Nixie thought, flicking her tail.

"Cool!" Jetty said.

"I'd love to see the magical ponies!" Nixie turned to Rip. "Let's go!"

Rip swam back a few feet and shook his head. "Nixie, no. Mermaids are forbidden from interacting with humans. You know the rules."

Nixie sighed. "That's an ancient rule that

makes no sense. Humans know merpeople exist."

"But you're supposed to avoid each other, to prevent humans and mermaids from becoming too interested in each other's worlds. That could lead to disaster. All of you merchildren must stay here." He turned to the other seaponies. "We're only supposed to patrol the river, since it connects to the ocean. Seaponies aren't meant to be friends with earth ponies. You can't rush up there every time you hear them singing."

Marina bowed her head. "I think it's important to be friends with them. They could let us know about any dangers headed our way."

"Yeah," Jetty said. "Come on, let's go through the portal."

"We pass right through it to the river," Marina said. "It doesn't take long."

"No, we should all stay here," Rip said.

The seaponies and merkids grumbled and frowned.

"Hey, let's hunt for the Kraken's Cave!" Cali said, rubbing her hands together. "Maybe we can get some of his treasure."

"That's just a silly myth," Rip said. "There's no Kraken. And there's no treasure to be found."

Nixie shrugged. "It might be fun just to go along. Maybe we could stop at the hot springs!"

Rip shook his head. "No, it's been a long day. Why don't you climb on and I'll take you home so you don't have to swim all that way?" he said to Nixie. "As you know, I'm rather fast." He winked.

"Okay, I guess. Thanks." She really didn't want a ride from him, but she had to get used to being his partner. *A team takes two*, she reminded herself. And he'd be moving in to her castle after the ceremony. She turned to Cali. "I'll see you tomorrow."

"Bye, Nixie," Cali said softly.

Nixie looped her arms around Rip's neck and he headed toward her castle. "We have to look out for each other," Rip said as he zoomed through the water. "I worry you aren't always . . . cautious."

Nixie's jaw dropped. "Well, you—" She snapped her mouth shut. She wasn't going to get in a fight with her new partner on the very first day.

Rip really was fast. Schools of tiny fish tried racing him, but he flew past them. In just minutes they were at her family's enormous sandcastle. The biggest in all of the Eastern Kingdoms. It was surrounded by bright, colorful coral fans and all types of

exotic sea plants. Normally, seeing it made her smile. But not today.

"Want to play fetch for a while?" Nixie knew Rip loved fetch.

"No. We need to rest up for tomorrow," he said. "I want to get together early."

"Early?"

"We should meet before the ceremony and review the rule book. I want us to be the best team in the history of the Rescue Crew."

Nixie sighed. "Okay. I'll meet you in the castle courtyard before lunch."

"How about before breakfast?" Rip asked.

"After breakfast."

"Very well. See you then—partner." He zipped off and Nixie blinked back tears. Rip meant well, but they just didn't click.

Chapter 5

Nixie needed to see her friends. So instead of going home, she swam to Piper's pretty conch shell house on the edge of the coral reef.

"Hello, dear!" Piper's dad said. "Congratulations."

"Thanks," Nixie said, wishing she could sound more excited. "Is Piper here? I didn't see her at the ceremony."

"She and Shelby are off on some adventure," he said. "They hoped to make it back

in time, but they didn't. I'll tell her you stopped by when she gets home."

Nixie nodded. This was supposed to be one of the happiest times of her life, and instead she was sadder than she'd ever been.

Nixie swam home and up to the room she'd decorated for her new seapony. For

Rip. She looked around at the carefully selected treasures: some of her favorite shells, a big cozy bed, pots of plants to nibble on. There was even a mural of the Eastern Kingdoms on the wall. She loved the room, but right now it made her frown.

"Rip probably won't like it," she said to herself. "We don't seem to agree on anything."

Nixie went next door to her own room. She sat on the balcony and scattered seaweed flakes in the water. The jellyfish from her presentation appeared and snatched them up. Watching them bob and sway in the water relaxed her. If she sang to them, they'd still dance. But she was too sad to sing.

She went inside and examined her jars of sea glass, her favorite ocean treasure, but even that didn't cheer her up.

That night, Nixie tossed and turned in bed. But she woke up early, determined to snap out of her bad mood. She had a kelp shake for breakfast and swam to the surface to watch the clouds before Rip came over. She loved feeling the sea breeze on her face and watching the birds fly past. Why had she agreed to study on a day meant for parties and celebration?

She swished her tail through the water, still trying to find a way to make this partnership work. She wouldn't have to spend all her time with Rip. She could still have moments to herself like this. And maybe they would make a very good team. That was the most important thing.

Rip's head popped up from below. "What are you doing?"

She slapped her tail against the water. "You scared me!"

"You shouldn't come to the surface without me. What if there was trouble?" Rip asked.

"We're in the protected part of the sea. Humans have agreed not to come to these waters," Nixie reminded him.

"What about whales? Sharks?"

"Then I'd use my shell. We can call for help, too, you know."

Rip rolled his eyes. "Of course I know that. Let's go study. Grab on. I'll take you back to the castle."

"I'd like to swim myself," Nixie snapped.

"Fine. I'll beat you there!" Rip zipped off and Nixie slowly swam back to the capital city.

Rip already had a book open when she got to the courtyard. "Let's review what to do if we ever run into sharks."

"I've never seen a shark in my life," Nixie said. "The coral reefs around the city keep them away."

"When we venture out of the city on rescues, we might encounter one." Rip cleared his throat. "Now, it's important to note that sharks don't speak the Mer language, so if you aren't wearing your Say Shell to translate, you won't be able to understand them."

"Do you really think they'd stop to chat?" Nixie asked.

"Probably not. But it is the first order of protocol to try to communicate. Next would be to distract them, perhaps with something shiny."

Nixie closed the book. "Rip, this was a good start. But I have so much to do to get ready. We'll have lots of time after this weekend to review rules and regulations."

"Very true." Rip picked up the book with his mouth and dropped it in his saddlebag. "I can't wait to get this pesky party over with so we can get to work."

After he left, Nixie swam to Shelby's house, but she wasn't home. Piper was out again, too. Where were they? Didn't they want to be friends anymore? They were supposed to help her get ready.

Luckily, Cascadia was there to keep Nixie company, and she spent hours weaving tiny braids throughout Nixie's long hair. They were twined with strings of pink pearls. It looked amazing.

Nixie got her special celebration outfit from the closet. Her shirt had strands of real silver. Her cape was a lovely blue, which looked wonderful against her shiny purple hair.

"Ready for your crown?" Cascadia asked.

Nixie smiled. "Yes." She loved her ceremonial crown. Normally she wore a small tiara. But her official crown was gorgeous. A giant pink sea gem was surrounded by starfish, coral, pink whelk shells, and bits of sea glass. Strands of pearls were looped around the base.

Cascadia placed it on her head. "This is so exciting. After tonight's ceremony, you can

go on rescue missions! I can't wait to go on one with you."

Nixie tried to imagine herself on an actual mission with Rip. He'd probably stop to read a rule book every two minutes.

She forced a smile. She was unhappy about Rip and disappointed her friends hadn't made time for her.

But she was *not* going to cry on Match Ceremony day.

Chapter 6

Nixie lined up with the rest of the royal merchildren and their seaponies outside the castle ballroom. Her friends were joking and having fun with their new partners. Rip floated beside her, saying nothing.

Is he having second thoughts, too? she wondered.

The doors to the ballroom opened and Principal Vanora and Headmaster Caspian greeted the crowd. "Welcome to our celebration!" Principal Vanora said. "At the stroke of midnight, when the full moon is high in the sky above the sea, we will officially join our royal merchildren with their magical seapony partners as members of the Royal Mermaid Rescue Crew."

That's when Nixie and Rip would recite the Rescue Crew oath and she'd get her rescue shell. It felt like minnows were back in her tummy.

"And now, introducing this year's Rescue Crew class!" Headmaster Caspian said.

The trumpet fish started playing music. Luminescent jellyfish bobbed along the ceiling, lighting up the room.

The merchildren and seaponies were greeted with whistles and applause. Waiters held trays of food and drinks. Tables were filled with presents for them. Nixie really wanted to be more excited than she felt.

"Eat, drink, dance!" Principal Vanora said. "Enjoy the party."

Nixie spotted a huge group of seaponies rushing toward them. "Is that your family?"

"Yes," Rip said. "I can't believe they all came. It is a very long journey to get here."

"We're so proud, son," said his father.

"Thanks," Rip said quietly. "Hey, Mack!" Rip nudged snouts with a smaller seapony.

"This is so cool!" Mack said. "I want to be a rescue seapony someday, too."

Everyone chuckled. Mack didn't have the glittery fins that marked all magical seaponies.

Mack pouted. "Stop laughing. It's not funny. My fins could turn glittery any day now."

Nixie knew that seaponies were either born glittery or not. "I'm sure you'd be great on a mission," she told Mack sincerely.

"You definitely would, buddy," Rip said. "But Mom and Dad need you to help out at home now that I'm not there."

"Helping with all the babies is so boring," Mack said. "It's not fair."

"Our little brothers and sisters look up to you. They need you."

The tiny seaponies swirled around Rip and Nixie. She giggled. "You guys are tickling me!"

"A real live princess!" one of them squeaked.

Rip whistled the loudest whistle Nixie had ever heard. All of the tiny seaponies immediately formed a circle. "Children! What do we say?"

"We're a big group, so stay in the loop!" the tiny seaponies chanted.

Wow, he's even strict with the little babies, Nixie thought.

"We're so pleased Rip is going to be your partner, Nixie," his mother said. "What a great team you'll make."

Nixie just smiled, because she didn't know what to say.

Cali swam up and grabbed Nixie's hand. "Let's dance."

Nixie turned to Rip. "Want to come?"

"I don't dance," he said.

"But all seaponies love music!" Nixie said. Would the two of them ever have fun together?

"I'll dance!" Mack said. "I love dancing. And this is a party!"

"You stay here so you don't get lost," Rip said.

Mack pouted and Nixie swam off.

Cali and her seapony, Rio, twirled on the dance floor. Cruise joined them with Jetty. Cali and Cruise's identical silver tails shimmered. They bickered sometimes, but they always had a lot of fun together.

Then Laguna grabbed Prince Dorado with her long tail and spun him around. All of the royal merchildren were dancing with

their seaponies—except for Nixie. She felt
so alone.

Luckily, Cascadia swam up and grabbed
her hand. They started dancing. "Why are
you by yourself?" Cascadia asked.

"Rip doesn't dance. He got me up early
to study this morning and says I shouldn't

float on the surface." Nixie sighed. "I tried getting to know him, but it didn't make things better at all."

"It's not too late to back out," Cascadia said softly. "The partnership can't be undone once you go through with it."

Nixie sighed. For years, she had dreamed about how much fun it would be to finally get paired with a magical seapony. She'd planned out adventures they'd have and secrets they'd share in between daring rescues. She just couldn't imagine those things with Rip.

"Do all the royal merkids you know absolutely love their seaponies?" Nixie asked.

"They do. I love Periwinkle. She's one of my best friends. I'd do anything for her. And she'd do anything for me," Cascadia said.

Nixie couldn't imagine feeling that way about Rip. "I need some time to think."

Cascadia hugged her. "Good luck, my sweet sister."

Nixie swam over to the table holding the rescue shells they'd soon be wearing. Every time she was summoned for a rescue, Rip would be joining her.

Unless she decided to cancel the match.

A rescue cape for each merchild hung next to the table. Inside, pockets and straps held tools and gear to use on rescues. Nixie's heart was pounding. What should she do?

"Help us!" a voice cried faintly from the shells. She might not have even heard it if they hadn't all been transmitting the same sound.

Nixie looked for Cascadia and other members of the Rescue Crew. Why weren't they rushing out the door? No one seemed to be hearing the message from their shells.

"Help!" the voice cried again, louder this time.

Nixie knew that voice!

Chapter 7

Nixie grabbed a rescue shell and went outside. "Piper, is that you?"

"Nixie, thank goodness! No one's been answering our call!" Piper said through the shell.

"I can barely hear you!" Nixie said.

"After I pressed the button to open the rescue channel, I dropped my shell," Piper said.

That explains why her voice sounds so far

away, Nixie thought. "What's wrong? Where are you?"

"We're on the other side of the kelp forest."

"By the rift?" Nixie shouted.

"Yes. Shelby hit her head and she's lying on the ground. She's not answering me. And I'm stuck in a coral reef. I can't help her."

"Oh no! How did that happen? Why are you there? I thought you'd be at the party." Nixie forgot all about being mad at her friends—now she was worried.

"It's a long story. Can you help us?" Piper asked.

"Of course," Nixie quickly said.

"We're going to get in so much trouble," Piper said.

"Not if no one knows what happened. I'll come by myself."

Rip would never agree to this mission. But Nixie could do this. She'd get there, check out the situation, and swish a fix.

"I'm on my way." She couldn't go back for a rescue cape. Someone might see her and try to stop her. That was okay, though—this wasn't official rescue business. She just needed to help her friends.

Nixie had never seen the rift, but she knew where it was. She had to swim over the oyster beds and through the kelp forest to get there.

She swam through the center of the city, past the Rescue Crew School. Then she passed over quiet streets of conch houses. She rarely went this far by herself. The ocean floor was still. Just a few starfish lounged on the sandy bottom. A school of bright little fish scattered right in front of her and she jumped, startled. Nixie repeated the rescue motto to herself: *On my honor, I will be brave as I keep our seas and subjects safe.*

She was getting closer to the rift. The ocean floor was soon covered with mounds of wavy gray oyster shells. Behind the beds, tall strands of giant kelp swayed in the current, as if they were beckoning a merperson to come in and stay for a while. Or forever. Merfolk were said to have gotten lost in the kelp forest for days. Even weeks. The kelp was so mesmerizing, Nixie had to snap her head away to stop looking at it.

She grabbed the rescue shell around her neck. "I'm here."

"Thank goodness!" Piper's voice was a little louder now that Nixie was closer.

"Yell so I can swim to where you are," Nixie instructed.

"We're over here!" Piper yelled. "Over here!"

"Okay, I'm coming through." Nixie took a deep breath before she went into the kelp forest.

She slipped between the long blades, trying her best to ignore the way they brushed up against her face. They slithered against her arms and she shivered. She thrashed her tail, but that only made them move more. She was starting to panic. What could she do? There had to be a solution.

She spotted an old branch sticking out of the sand. She pulled it out and used it to push aside the kelp as she swam. It was much easier. "Keep shouting so I can swim toward you!" she called.

"I'm over here!" Piper hollered. "Over here!"

Nixie wanted to be angry that her friends had ignored the biggest weekend of her life and gone off on this crazy adventure. But they were in trouble. This was no time for a lecture. That was something Rip would do.

Finally, she swam out of the forest.

"Thank goodness you're here!" Piper said. She was wedged in a hole in a coral formation. Shelby was lying on the sand nearby. There was a bag on the ground next to Piper.

Nixie hurried over to Shelby. She reached for her limp hand. "Can you hear me?"

Shelby didn't answer.

"She tried to pull me out of here, but she lost her grip and flew back in the water. She hit her head on a rock," Piper explained.

Nixie dropped Shelby's hand and swam back to Piper. "How did you get stuck in there?"

Piper hung her head. "We've been searching for sea glass all week. To give to you for a present, at your party."

Nixie's eyes widened. "So that's where you've been? I thought . . . I thought maybe you guys didn't want to be friends anymore."

"Why would you think that?"

"Because I'm going to be busier now," Nixie said. "Because the Rescue Crew is going to be such a big part of my life." *That is, if I become a member tonight.*

"We'll always be friends with you, Nixie. We're excited for you!" Piper said.

Nixie smiled, relieved. "But why did you come all the way out here?"

"We've been looking everywhere for sea glass. I figured there would be tons of it on the other side of the kelp forest. No one swims out here. I didn't realize we were so close to the rift," Piper said.

"And how did you get stuck?" Nixie asked.

Brightly colored fish swam around the reef poking around for food, like a stuck mergirl was no problem at all.

Piper frowned. "I saw a really sparkly piece of sea glass in this formation. I swam in to get it but got stuck on the way out. And I dropped the piece of glass."

"Don't worry about that. I'm going to free you first, so you can help me carry Shelby out," Nixie said.

"Where's your seapony?" Piper asked.

"It's a long story." Nixie swam around the formation to figure out how to get Piper out. What she saw made her want to swim back to the castle. The deep, murky rift was scarily close. The ocean bottom just disappeared into . . . darkness.

Chapter 8

Nixie was so scared, her teeth were chattering. But she couldn't let Piper know how frightened she was. Keeping calm was one of the top rules for the Rescue Crew. And her two best friends were in danger! She had to find a way to handle this.

Schools of fish swam overhead, and there were so many beautiful types of coral. It was an amazing spot. Too bad it was also really dangerous. Hopefully, she'd never have to come back here again.

Nixie spotted a big hole on the other side of the formation. Piper would be able to swim out of it. But it was right next to the rift! Still, it was a way out. "Piper, can you slide back down into the formation?"

"I think so," Piper said.

"Good. Because there's another way out on the other side." If Nixie could keep Piper's back facing the rift, Piper wouldn't get scared. Nixie stuck her head in the big hole in the coral. "I'm over here, can you hear me?"

"Yes, but I'm still stuck," Piper said.

"Try wriggling down," Nixie told her.

Piper flicked her tail, but she didn't budge. "It's not working."

"Stop!" Rip was next to the formation.

Nixie looked up, stunned. "What are you doing here?"

Rip swam closer. "Mack was hanging around outside the castle and heard you talking about a rescue mission! He heard everything. We're supposed to be partners. A team takes two! Why didn't you call me?"

Nixie balled up her fists. "Because you would have stopped me!"

"Of course I would have! We're not even officially Rescue Crew members yet. We're not supposed to be on a mission—especially to such a dangerous location! The rift is right behind you! No one even knows for sure what kinds of creatures are down there. They could be watching us from the deep as we speak!"

Nixie gritted her teeth. "These are my *friends*. They'll get in big trouble if anyone knows they came out here. I had to find them. I know what I'm doing. And I don't need your help."

Rip frowned. "Of course you need my help. I've read the entire rule book twice. You haven't even finished it yet."

Nixie rolled her eyes. "Rules aren't the only thing needed in a rescue. And as it turns out, I've already swished a fix for this one."

Rip tilted his head. "Swished a fix? What does that mean?"

"It means she's thinking of a great idea," Piper said from the formation. "Which she does all the time!"

"I don't understand," Rip said.

Nixie felt her cheeks burning. "It means I come up with a plan—that might not be in the rule book. I swish my tail around when I'm thinking about a problem. When I'm coming up with a fix for it." She shrugged. "I swish a fix."

"Oh, Nixie. Is that how you came up with your jellyfish project?" Rip laughed. "Swishing a fix is not a real thing!"

"Of course it is," Nixie said. "I do it all the time, and I always find a great answer to my problem."

"We find great answers in our books, not by flipping our tails around. Let me get my book out and do some research." Rip flipped open his saddlebag with his snout and grabbed his book. A small seapony zoomed up behind him. Rip's eyes went wide. "Mack! What are you doing?"

"I wanted to come along on the mission," Mack said. "I might be able to help."

"Of course you can't help. You're not a trained Rescue Crew member."

"I'm sure bringing him is against the rules," Nixie said.

"It most definitely is. But I didn't bring him. He snuck along behind me," Rip said angrily.

"Hey, you wouldn't even be here if it wasn't for me," Mack said.

"Go back toward the kelp curtain and stay out of the way. This is a very dangerous mission and I don't want you to get hurt," Rip said.

"I'm smart and I'm brave," Mack said.

"But you haven't read our schoolbooks, either," Rip said. "Wait by the kelp!"

Grumbling, Mack swam away from them.

"Now, let me look through the book and figure out what to do," Rip said.

"There isn't time for that!" Nixie said. "Shelby is hurt, and I already have a plan. We're figuring it out as we go."

"That's not how we're going to do rescue missions in the future," Rip said.

Nixie bit her lip, but she couldn't hold back her anger. "That's fine, because I don't want to be your partner anyway! I never did!"

Chapter 9

Rip said nothing for a few moments. "What do you mean? At the selection ceremony, you said you were hoping to pick me."

Nixie hung her head, instantly regretting that she'd told him the truth. But it was clear they were a terrible match! "I said that because I didn't want you to feel bad for getting picked last."

Rip blinked a few times. "So you didn't want me for a partner? Why not?"

Nixie sighed. "We're very different. All you care about are the rules!"

"When you have dozens of little brothers and sisters to watch over, you need rules to make things run smoothly! To keep everyone safe. There are rules for a reason, Nixie, and we have to follow them."

"And sometimes rules are meant to be broken. You can't seem to understand that."

Rip nodded slowly. "I suppose we have to face the truth. You know, one rule says we can back out of tonight's ceremony. We don't have to become partners."

"I do know about that rule," Nixie said softly. "But right now I have to rescue my friends. Don't worry, I've already figured everything out. Watch your brother and I'll get to work," Nixie said. "If you don't help me, then technically you're not breaking the rules." She swam toward Piper, feeling horrible but determined.

Rip didn't follow. He swam toward the kelp.

"We've got to hurry and get Shelby," Piper said. "It's going to get dark soon."

"I'll swim into the formation and try to pull you down," Nixie said, focusing on her friend.

"Hurry!" Piper said.

Nixie swam to Piper and tried grabbing on to her tail, but she couldn't get a good grip. "I'm going to have to break away some of the coral around you." Nixie got a rock from the ocean floor and whacked it against the coral trapping Piper. A small bit broke off, and Piper slid down into the formation.

"Good thinking!" Piper said.

That was the easy part, Nixie thought, knowing they were going to have to swim over the spooky rift to get out. "Follow me!"

Nixie swam out of the hole. Her tail was hanging right above the rift. She made sure not to look down. She gripped the coral and stuck her head back in the hole. "This way, Piper!"

Piper swam toward her, then stopped. "Hey! I found that cool piece of sea glass." She swam next to Nixie and held out her palm. In it was a shiny blue heart.

Nixie picked it up and examined it. It felt heavier than a piece of glass. "I don't think this is sea glass."

"What is it, then?" Piper asked.

Nixie couldn't believe it. "I think this is the Sea Diamond from the Trident of Protection! It's the same shape and the same color! Hang on to it. We'll show it to the principal and see what she thinks." Nixie handed it back to Piper. "Now let's get Shelby. Swim out, and then turn around so you're facing the kelp curtain. Don't look behind you. And don't drop that Sea Diamond!"

Piper swam out, but she looked over her shoulder. She screamed.

Nixie couldn't blame her for being scared. Nixie tried to sound calm. "Don't worry.

The rift is just a deep drop. We're not going to fall in."

"I'm not scared of that!" Piper yelled. "I'm scared of the shark!"

Nixie turned around and saw a big gray beast headed straight for them.

Chapter 10

Nixie grabbed Piper's hand. Rip was fast enough to outswim the shark, but he wasn't there. Oh, why had she told him she didn't need his help?

The girls tried swimming away, but the shark was right in front of them, pinning them against the reef. Nixie had no idea what to do. No amount of tail swishing could fix this. Everything she'd learned at the academy vanished from her mind. *Think, think!*

Breathe, focus, solve, she reminded herself. Nixie took a deep breath as the shark stared them down. She could feel Piper's hand trembling in hers. Focusing on the scene in front of her, she saw the shark's gills opening and closing as it swam back and forth in front of them. She wasn't wearing her Say Shell, so she couldn't talk to it. If only she had reviewed that chapter on sharks with Rip earlier that morning!

Solve this! What are my options, what can I do? What did Rip say about encountering sharks? Distract them with something shiny! What did she have that was shiny? "Throw the diamond into the rift!"

"No! That's your gift!" Piper said.

"You're more important than a diamond.

Now throw it! It might distract him. It's the only option!" Nixie screamed.

Piper held the diamond up so the shark could see it and then hurled it toward the abyss. The shark turned and swam after it.

"It worked!" Nixie shouted. "Now let's get Shelby!"

Piper grabbed the bag of sea glass as they rushed around the reef toward Shelby. She was lying on the ground. "She's still unconscious," Nixie said. Nixie and Piper each wrapped an arm around her.

Rip swam up beside them. "I know you don't want my help, but you need it. Grab on and I'll speed through the kelp forest."

"Thank you," Nixie said quietly.

She and Piper pulled Shelby up. Then Nixie grabbed on to Rip's neck. "Let's go!"

They headed for the edge of the kelp forest, where they stopped to get Mack.

"Hold on to my tail!" Rip said. Then he charged headfirst through the tall, swaying plants.

Nixie kept her eyes closed as they swam. She thought it would be less scary that way, if she couldn't see the weeds. But it was even worse feeling them slither across her skin in the dark.

Then—*yank!* One of the plants wrapped around her wrist and jerked her away from Shelby and Rip.

"Help! I'm caught!" Nixie thrashed around, but that only made things worse. Now she was tangled up in several strands.

"You'll be fine," Rip said calmly. "Let me get Piper, Shelby, and Mack out of the kelp, and then I'll be back for you." He shot out of the forest, and in just a few moments he was swimming back to her. But he was going so fast, he didn't notice one of the long, green ropes had tied him up, too.

Chapter 11

"What do we do?" Nixie asked. "I don't remember studying this."

"We haven't yet," Rip said. "But luckily I've read ahead. Kelp is thick, but you can cut through it. In this scenario, we would try our rescue tools—if we had our gear, which we don't, since we aren't officially crew members yet and shouldn't be here." He paused. "So actually, I'm not sure what to do. Perhaps we should use your rescue shell to call the crew members to get us."

"No, we're not asking for help. We can figure this out." Nixie's mind spun. She swished her tail, thinking. What could she use that was like a knife? "Mack!" she shouted. "Can you please bring me two empty oyster shells?"

"Mack, no! You're too little to get involved!" Rip yelled.

"He's just the right size," Nixie said. "He'll be able to dart through this kelp with no problem."

"You want me to help with your mission?" Mack asked from the other side of the kelp curtain.

"We sure do," Nixie said.

"Cool! I'll be right there," Mack shouted.

"I don't like this one bit. I've lost track of how many rules we're breaking," Rip said, struggling against the ropes of kelp.

"Relax, we've got this," Nixie said.

Mack scooted right through the kelp and brought two shells to Nixie. "What are you going to do?" he asked.

"Watch." She smashed the shells together and they broke. The edges were jagged and sharp, like a knife. She started sawing through the plant. "Mack, use your snout to try and loosen some of Rip's knots."

"I'm on it!" Mack swam over to Rip and started untying him.

It didn't take long for Nixie to free herself. She swam over to Rip and used her shell
to cut through one last kelp strand.

"We did it!" Mack yelled.

"Yeah!" Nixie hollered.

Rip shook off the loose kelp strands. "So
that's swishing a fix. Nixie, I'm impressed.

That was very well done. You freed us without using any techniques from the rule book."

"Well, you're the one who knew that our tools could cut through this. That's how I thought of using broken shells." Nixie smiled at him, and Rip smiled back.

Carefully, they swam through the kelp and got to the other side.

Piper hugged Nixie. "Thank goodness you're okay."

"What's happening?" Shelby sat up, rubbing her head. "Nixie, what are you doing here?"

"She's missing her party," Piper said. "We had to be rescued."

"Do we still have her present?" Shelby asked.

Piper nodded. "She knows about the sea glass. But we lost the special piece I was trying to get."

"What happened?" Shelby asked.

Piper and Nixie laughed. "It's a long story. We'll tell you later. Are you feeling okay?"

"Yes. I just have a bit of a headache," Shelby said. "I'll feel better when I get something to eat and drink."

"We should get back," Nixie said. "Everyone will be wondering where we are."

"Yes, and it's getting dark. Fortunately, I've been working on a spell to illuminate rocks. Can you grab one?" Rip asked her.

Nixie plucked a rock from the ocean floor.

Rip cleared his throat and fluttered his glittery fins. "Let this rock glow, bright light please show." The chunk lit up.

"Wow!" Mack said.

Nixie was impressed. "I've only seen the very simplest of spells from the other sea-ponies in class."

"I've been practicing some spells on my own time," Rip said.

Nixie gulped. She'd been so busy concentrating on the things she didn't like about Rip that she hadn't realized how smart he really was. How hard he worked. How very calm and confident he was on a mission.

"Everyone, hang on and I'll get us back in no time," Rip said. "Nixie, hold up that glow stone."

Nixie held up the rock while everyone else grabbed hold of Rip's saddlebag. He shot through the water, and Nixie realized the thrill she was feeling was exactly what she had always imagined a rescue would be like with her perfect seapony match.

Chapter 12

They swam back to the castle and saw two figures outside.

"Oh no. It's the principal and headmaster!" Nixie said.

"So much for sneaking off and not getting caught," Rip said.

"There you are!" Principal Vanora said. "We're just about to start the ceremony. Where have you been?"

Nixie and Rip looked at each other.

"We went on a rescue mission," Nixie admitted, right as Rip said, "We were off getting to know each other better."

Nixie and Rip looked at each other again and laughed.

"I figured you wouldn't tell," Rip said.

Nixie shrugged. "And I figured you would."

"I'm confused," Headmaster Caspian said. "You went on a mission? An actual rescue?"

Nixie nodded yes and explained what had happened.

Principal Vanora shook her head in disbelief. "You're very lucky you didn't get hurt. We can't let this go unpunished. I think a complete review of our rule book is in order. And you'll do it tomorrow."

"Excellent idea!" Nixie and Rip said together.

Principal Vanora turned to Piper and Shelby. "I hope you at least collected some great sea glass."

Shelby nodded and opened her bag. "We found a bunch."

"But we lost the most beautiful piece. That's how I got stuck," Piper said.

"It wasn't just a beautiful piece of sea glass," Nixie said. "I think it was the Sea Diamond from the Trident of Protection."

The principal gasped. "What? Are you serious?"

Nixie nodded. "It was heavy. And it was light blue and shaped like a heart. Just like in the old stories."

"What a shame you lost it," the headmaster said.

"Mack, check my saddlebag," Rip said.

Mack stuck his head in the bag. He came out holding a shiny blue heart in his mouth.

"The Sea Diamond!" Nixie was stunned. "But we saw the shark go after it—over the rift!"

"I'm fast, remember? And I like to play fetch." Rip smiled. "When you told me to stay behind, I didn't listen. I heard you say it could be the Sea Diamond, so I knew to go after it. Then we were so busy getting out of that kelp forest, I forgot to tell you about it."

Principal Vanora held out her hand and Mack placed the stone in her palm. "I can't believe it. This is the Sea Diamond."

"Unfortunately, it's useless on its own," the headmaster said. "The Fathom Pearl and the Night Star are still missing. And the trident itself is gone."

"But if the Sea Diamond was found, maybe the rest weren't swept into the rift, either," the principal said. "Rip, may I keep this in a safe place?"

"Of course," Rip said. "And I'll be sure to keep my eyes open for the rest of the gems."

"Yes, we'll have to review that tale in class next week so others can be on the lookout as well," the headmaster said.

"I see you've got your rescue shell already, Nixie," Principal Vanora said. "Let's all get inside. We need to prepare for the ceremony." She swam into the castle.

"I'm glad you children are all right," the headmaster said. "Girls, I'll call the merdoctor to look you over."

Piper and Shelby waved to Nixie. "See you soon!"

"I'm going to find Mom and Dad and tell them everything!" Mack swam off.

Nixie and Rip were alone. "So, if you hand your rescue shell back to the principal, you can wait until the next selection ceremony to choose another seapony," Rip told her.

Nixie's heart hurt. "I know that."

"Is that what you're going to do?" Rip asked.

Nixie suddenly knew what she had to do. What she wanted to do. She threw her arms around Rip's neck. "No, I'm not going to hand my shell back. I don't want another seapony. You're smart and brave and loyal. You tried

to keep me out of trouble—and you didn't even tell a lie to do it. We *were* getting to know each other."

Rip grinned. "Guess I swished a good fix there, huh?"

Nixie laughed. "You sure did. But are you sure *you* want to be paired with *me*?"

"Absolutely. A team takes two and turns out, we're a great one. With your creativity, and my complete understanding of the rules and tactics to use, I think we really will be the best team in the history of the Rescue Crew," Rip said. "It felt great working with you. Just like I always imagined it would be."

Nixie grinned. "I know what you mean. Now let's get inside for the ceremony!"

"Climb on!" Rip said.

Chapter 13

As Nixie and Rip swam into the ballroom, Cascadia waved to her sister. "I'll be right back," Nixie told Rip.

"What's going on?" Cascadia asked. "You two look like you're getting along well."

Nixie smiled. "We are. Everything is going to be all right. Rip is a great partner!" She quickly told her what had happened.

"A rescue already? I can't believe it. I'm so happy it all worked out." Cascadia hugged her, and Nixie got back in line with Rip. Her stomach felt like it was full of minnows again, but this time, it was a good feeling. She was so excited to become an official member of the Rescue Crew!

The clock in the ballroom ticked to midnight and started chiming.

"Princes and princesses of the Eastern Kingdom, it is time to make your Rescue Crew partnership official. Please swim forward to receive your shells and capes and repeat the Rescue Crew oath."

Prince Cruise and Jetty went first. He took off his ceremonial cape and put on the shorter, red rescue cape made to wear on missions.

"On my honor, I will be brave as I keep our seas and subjects safe," Cruise and Jetty said in unison.

The crowd cheered.

Nixie watched proudly as the rest of her classmates were officially matched with their seaponies.

"Princess Nixie and Rip, please come forward and repeat the oath," Principal Vanora said.

"On my honor, I will be brave as I keep our seas and subjects safe," they said together.

"And we have a special commendation for a brave seapony who helped out with a situation earlier tonight. Mack, can you please join us onstage," the headmaster said.

Mack swam up and spun in circles, he was so excited. Everyone laughed.

"While you aren't a magical seapony," the headmaster said, "you are clever and helpful. Wear this shell as a reminder to be brave as you help keep your family safe. It's a very important job."

"Thanks!" Mack beamed.

"Let the celebrations continue!" Principal Vanora announced to great applause.

Everyone crowded the dance floor. Marina changed colors to match Lana's pink outfit. Cali and Cruise held hands, twirling and laughing. Dorado was bopping to the beat of the blowfish band.

Nixie wished Rip could dance, but that was okay. He could do so many other wonderful things. "I'll be back in a few minutes," she told him. "I just want to celebrate with my friends."

But before Nixie swam to the dance floor, Rip pulled her aside. "Can I ask a favor?"

"Sure!" Nixie said. "What is it?"

Rip sighed. "The reason I don't dance is because I can't. I don't know how. Can you teach me? Like you taught the jellyfish to dance in your presentation? Which technically weren't fish, but still. It was an impressive project."

Nixie blinked at him a few times. "You want to learn to dance? Seriously?"

He frowned. "I wanted to teach myself, but I couldn't find a book on dancing."

Nixie smiled. "Of course I'll teach you to dance—partner."

The adventures continue . . .

#2: Lana Swims North

"We're members of the Royal Mermaid Rescue Crew," Lana said. "Are you lost?"

"Not exactly," the creature said. "But I'm not entirely sure where I am."

Lana smiled. "That sounds a little bit like being lost. What's your name?"

"Spike. Because of my . . ." He rolled his eyes up to look at his horn. "I live in the Eastern Seas with a pod of dolphins. But I'm the only one with a horn."

"How magnificent!" Lana said.

"No, it's not. I keep poking other dolphins by mistake. I cut my best friend. They're not safe with me," Spike explained. "So I'm searching for a new home."

"We can help you," Lana said. "I live in the kingdom of Stillwater, north of here, but I'm spending the weekend in my dorm at the Rescue Crew School. Stay with us tonight!"

"Oh, thank you," Spike said. "I never thought I'd run into such helpful creatures."

A warm feeling spread through Lana's chest. Why couldn't being a Rescue Crew member always be like this?

Welcome to the
ENCHANTED PONY ACADEMY,
where dreams sparkle and magic shines!